STRAWBERRY

PENCIL MAGIC ®

Look
for
the
star! ™

"Peri And Her Plant"

Written By: Michael Girgenti

Illustrated By: Valiant Graphics

Peri lives on a big, beautiful farm with lots of cows and sheep.

Peri tries to play with these cows and sheep, but they ignore her. This makes Peri sad. Peri's only wish in the world is to have a friend.

Each and every day, Peri explores the farmyard for a playmate, but all the animals run away—even the frogs.

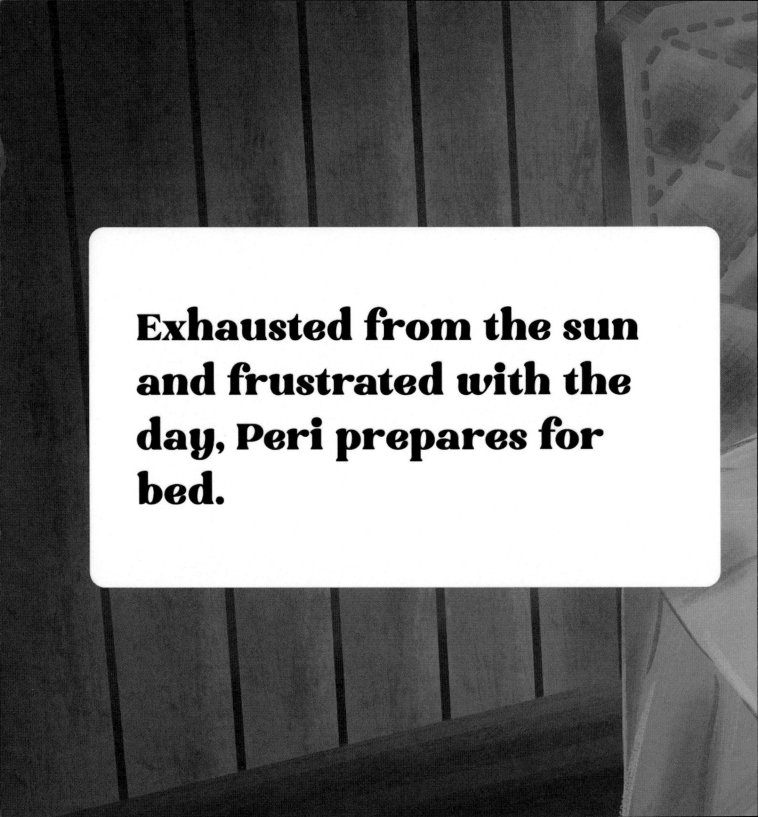

Exhausted from the sun and frustrated with the day, Peri prepares for bed.

With Peri's birthday only days away, this still does not seem to excite her. Peri's birthday is on Earth Day. Even on this special occasion Peri still feels lonely.

Peri's uncle, a local farmer, hands Peri a special box. Peri's eyes begin to glow. Inside this special box sits a small, special plant inside a small, special pot.

Peri, proud of this plant, waters it daily, keeping it perfectly in the sunlight as it slowly begins to grow. Peri, delighted with her new gift, seems to have found a new friend.

Peri, in utter glee, takes the plant with her everywhere. All the farm animals love it, even the frogs.

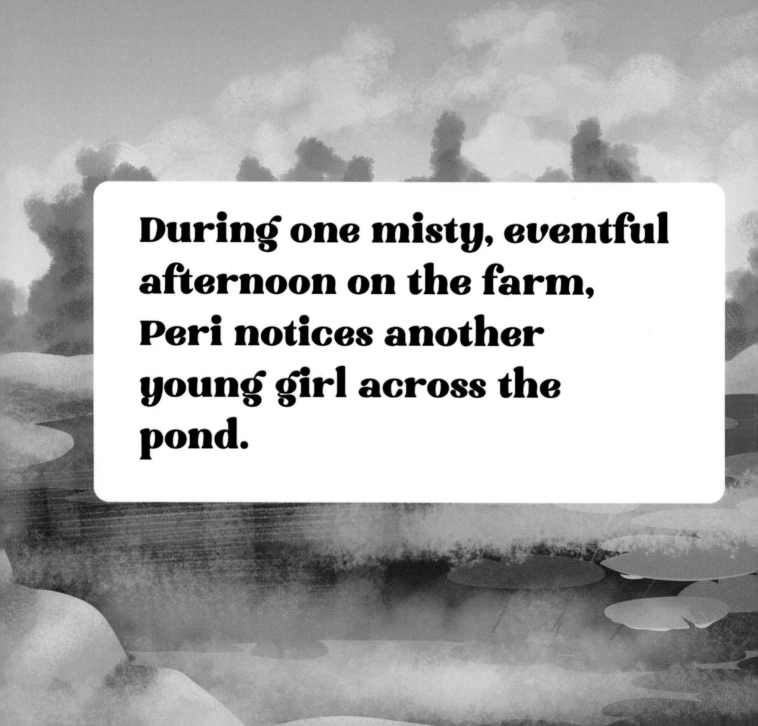

During one misty, eventful afternoon on the farm, Peri notices another young girl across the pond.

With her plant in hand, Peri walks over and introduces herself to the other girl. To Peri's surprise, the other girl also has a plant. Hers is a cactus.

Thrilled to meet someone else with similar interests, the other girl introduces herself to Peri as "Lavie." From that moment on, Peri and Lavie were the best of friends.

After greeting one another, Lavie suggests they explore into the woods together. The girls, in excitement, agree. The girls, after a mile, encounter a broken-glassed greenhouse that stands tall into the sky. Skeptical at first, they proceed to enter.

As the girls tiptoe around, they hear the very faint sound of singing from what seems to be a plant. The frightened girls immediately stop. No one is around or in sight.

Fearless Peri steps forward first to investigate. Upon her exploration, Peri discovers a unique snail with a stuffy nose inside a plant pot wearing a hat. Peri slowly reaches for a nearby garden tool, gently scooping up the mollusk and bringing it closer.

The snail calmly smiles at Peri, raising its chin and introducing itself as "Snotty." Before the girls can react or reply, Snotty the snail sneezes.

Snotty's sneeze has activated the greenhouse into a futuristic world learning center. Snotty rises above the girls into the air on an automatic, spinning, circular platform. "You both have been chosen by me, Snotty the snail."

The girls stand stunned as they listen to the snail continue to speak. "I will be assigning both of you the specific task of planting as many trees and flowers across the world as fast as you can, but you will need to work together to save our planet before it is too late."

The soft-spoken Peri proposes a simple question, "When would we start"?

Snotty smiles. "Today! Remember, the day you plant the seed is not the day you eat the fruit. Together, over time, we will overcome anything! Now take these..." Out of thin air, magical watches appear and float in front of the girls.

The girls reach for their watches and connect the gadgets to their wrists. An alarm begins to sound. "Now go change the world, my girls!" screeched Snotty as the greenhouse reverses and warps back to normal.

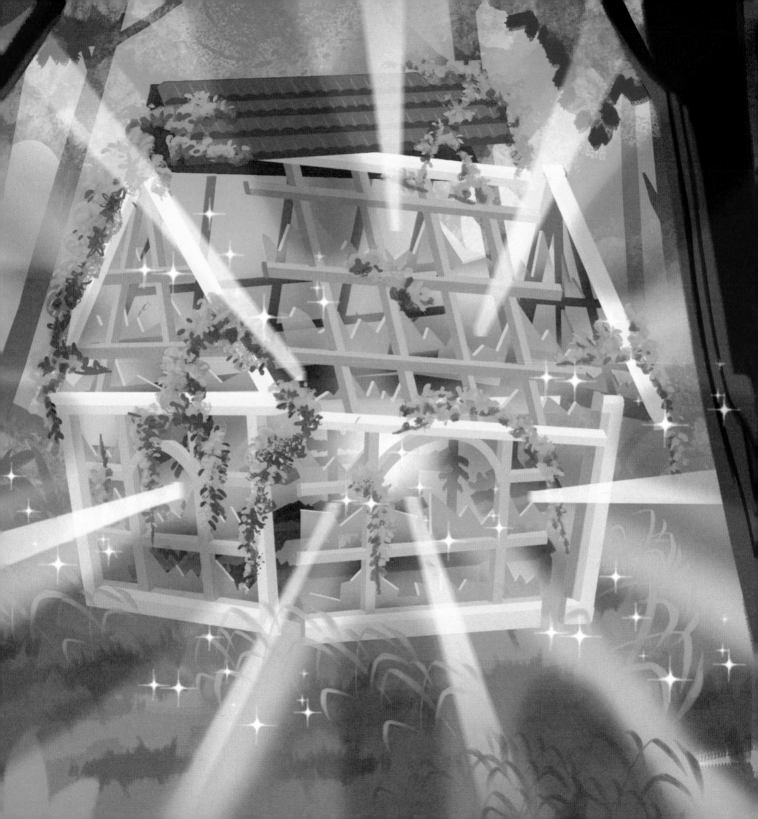

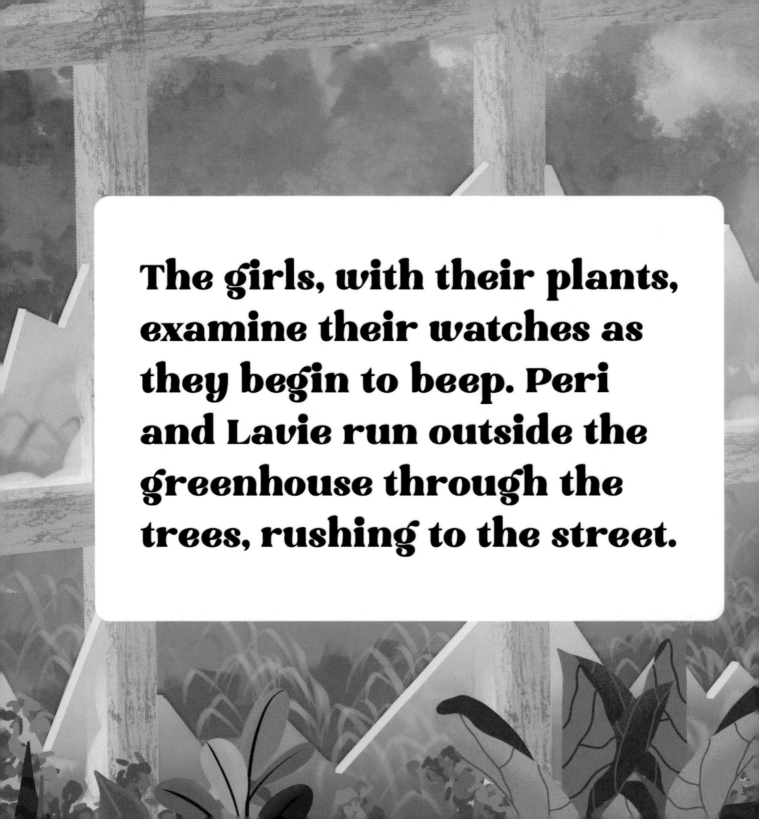

The girls, with their plants, examine their watches as they begin to beep. Peri and Lavie run outside the greenhouse through the trees, rushing to the street.

A flower planting machine awaits them with their names flashing across the screen. The girls enter the self-driving machine and begin to plant trees, flowers, and seeds to the rhythmic beeping of Snotty's watch.

Slowly but surely, Peri and Lavie make the world greener, for Earth Day and for every day.